P9-BBP-973

GHOSTS, HAUNTINGS and MYSTERIOUS HAPPENINGS

Strange Unsolved Mysteries from Tor Books

Ghosts, Hauntings, and Mysterious Happenings
Mysteries of People and Places
Mysteries of Ships and Planes
Monsters, Strange Dreams, and UFOs

STRANGE UNSOLVED MYSTERIES

GHOSTS, HAUNTINGS and MYSTERIOUS HAPPENINGS

PHYLLIS
RAYBIN EMERT
Illustrated by
JAEL

TOR

A TOM DOHERTY ASSOCIATES BOOK
NEW YORK

GHOSTS, HAUNTINGS, AND MYSTERIOUS HAPPENINGS

Copyright © 1992 by RGA Publishing Group, Inc.

Cover and interior art by Jael

A Tor Book
Published by Tom Doherty Associates, Inc.
175 Fifth Avenue
New York, N.Y. 10010

Tor ® is a registered trademark of Tom Doherty Associates, Inc.

ISBN: 0-812-52057-2

First edition: September 1992

Printed in the United States of America

0 9 8 7 6 5 4 3 2

FOR JOSHUA BENJAMIN EMERT

Contents

Contents

The Whaley House

It's been called one of the most actively haunted houses in the world. The U.S. Chamber of Commerce and the State of California have officially recognized the Whaley House as a genuine haunted house!

Located in Old Town San Diego, the two-story mansion was built in 1856 by city pioneer Thomas Whaley. In addition to being the residence of the Whaley family, parts of the house were also used at various times as a county courthouse, a church, a post office, a public school, and home base for a theater group.

The last Whaley to live in the house was Lillian, who died in 1953 at the age of eighty-nine. Today, the house has been preserved as a historical museum and is open to the public.

Strange, unexplained incidents began happening in 1960. These were noted in detail by Jean Reading, the curator and chief historian of the Whaley House.

Footsteps, piano music, and rapping noises have been heard. Visitors have seen strange lights and moving objects. Some people have smelled strong odors of perfume or cigar smoke. Others have felt cold spots or mysterious touches. A number of people claim even to have seen actual ghosts!

One person reported seeing the figure of a small woman in a long hoop skirt. Another saw a man in old-fashioned dress. A ghost dog has been spotted from time to time, and the noises of a baby crying have been heard.

In the 1980s a young woman who worked as a tour guide at the Whaley House told everyone she wanted to see a real ghost.

"Be patient, Denise," said Jean Reading. "It can be dangerous saying things like that out loud in a house like this. The walls have ears," she added.

One Christmas, some visitors to the mansion heard the sound of footsteps. Jean and Denise went upstairs to investigate the vacant second floor.

In the main bedroom, the women discovered two windows wide open. I'm sure these were shut, thought Jean. Apparently, the horizontal bolts on the windows had been pulled back by unseen hands!

As they walked over to check on the nursery, a man's voice suddenly boomed out with laughter. Denise grew pale as she turned toward Jean, who stood frozen, unable to move a muscle.

Finally, Denise whispered, "Let's get out of here!" Both women bolted down the stairs.

Did they hear the laughter of Thomas Whaley? Maybe so, but the exact place where the mysterious event occurred was above the location of an old execution site. A man named Yankee Jim Robinson was hanged at that very spot on which the Whaley House was built!

If ever there was a restless and angry spirit, Jim Robinson was one. He had been arrested for stealing a boat and was sentenced to hang by a drunken judge. Jim didn't believe they would go through with the execution because it was much too harsh a sentence for the crime of theft. He thought it would be called off at the last second, but unfortunately, it wasn't.

To add insult to injury, Yankee Jim didn't die instantly of a broken neck, as do most victims of hanging. He dropped only a few feet and hung there for thirty to forty seconds before he finally strangled to death.

Some say the heavy footsteps heard in the Whaley House are those of the ghost of Yankee Jim Robinson.

The spirit of Thomas Whaley is also restless. When he was alive, part of his home was used as the county courthouse, and Whaley was paid sixty-five dollars a month for the privilege. The county records were stored there for several years.

But as time went by, large portions of the population of Old Town shifted to a new area, called New Town. The people of New Town wanted the courthouse moved to their area, but Thomas Whaley refused. The people of Old Town supported Whaley and vowed to fight the citizens of New Town.

When Whaley was away on a business trip, his opponents came to the house at midnight and forced their way in. Holding Mrs. Whaley at gunpoint, they took the county records and left.

When he returned, Whaley was infuriated at what had happened! For nineteen years he tried to get the county to pay the remaining months on their lease and reimburse him for repairs on the building required after the break-in. But the case was never settled. Whaley died in 1890, angry and bitter over the injustice of his situation.

Other ghosts haunt the mansion. The small woman seen by many visitors is probably Thomas's wife, Anna, who was only 4 feet 11 inches tall. The crying baby is very likely the spirit of seventeen-month-old Tom Whaley, the son of Thomas and Anna, who died in an upstairs room of the house.

4

Many have seen and been frightened by these strange incidents at the Whaley house, but no one has ever been harmed or injured. This well-documented haunted house continues to attract visitors year round.

The Haunted Battlefield

"Such a beautiful and peaceful-looking place," said the Englishwoman. She had ridden a bicycle from her hotel to the Scottish Highlands to see the Pass of Killiecrankie.

It's hard to believe this was the site of so much blood, pain, and death, she thought to herself. Surrounded by high cliffs, she gazed at the narrow, rocky valley below her. It was a lovely day, and not a cloud was in the bright blue sky.

As the afternoon wore on, the woman recalled the history of the area. In 1689, there was a terrible battle in the pass between English soldiers and Scottish Highlanders. The English had removed the Scottish King, James II, from the throne and replaced him with Mary and her husband, William of Orange. Scotland still supported James. At Killiecrankie, the Scots won a total victory over the British, slaughtering the Redcoats to the last man. After the battle, the Highlanders stripped the bodies of all valuables and killed any wounded.

Killiecrankie was the only victory for the Highlanders, who were eventually overwhelmed by the British forces.

The woman sat down in front of a tree and looked all around her. Does the land see and remember? she thought. I wonder.

It was fall, and as the sun dropped in the sky, the woman felt a chill in the air. She was so relaxed she didn't feel like moving.

I've got plenty of food in my picnic basket and a heavy coat, she thought. I think I'll spend the night here and bicycle back to the hotel in the morning.

She leaned back against the tree, closed her eyes, and eventually fell asleep. Hours later, she woke with a start. Was that faraway thunder she heard, or the sound of guns?

The moon was so bright that she could see by her watch that it was 2 A.M. Suddenly, she heard noises erupt throughout the valley below her. She watched as an unbelievable scene unfolded.

A large group of red-coated soldiers and their horses and pack mules gathered below. They groped for their guns and seemed to be in total disorder. When the woman looked up, she saw the reason for their confusion.

Swarms of Highlanders, screaming the name of James II, descended on the Redcoats. The huge band of Scottish warriors carried swords and shields against the English flintlock guns and bayonets.

Shrieks and cries filled the air as the British were slaughtered. Their guns were no match for the Scottish fighters. Horses panicked and soldiers begged for mercy, but there was none. Men were butchered and the ground turned red with their blood.

The woman was horrified and couldn't speak. The battle was totally one-sided. Finally, unable to watch any longer, she sobbed and covered her eyes. Then a silence fell over the valley.

Moments later she looked up. Bodies and limbs were strewn everywhere. A few men, still alive, moaned in pain while others simply cried. The Englishwoman smelled the scent of death in the air.

Living people moved among the bodies. They pulled the clothes off corpses, taking shoes, belts, and buttons. A young woman scavenger, carrying a basket and a dagger, did her work not far from the Englishwoman. One soldier, barely alive, moved slightly as the woman tried to take his wedding ring. Without hesitation, she bent forward and slit his throat.

The Englishwoman cried out. The scavenger

turned, looked directly into her eyes, and began moving slowly toward her.

"No! No!" the Englishwoman screamed in her mind, but she was so frozen with fear that she could not speak. As the young woman with the dagger leaned close, the Englishwoman lost consciousness.

When she opened her eyes it was daylight. She was alone and cold. The Pass of Killiecrankie was beautiful and peaceful once again. There was no sign of the bloodshed she had witnessed. Shivering, she slowly pulled herself up, climbed on her bicycle, and rode back to the hotel. When she told the staff what had happened, they nodded their heads.

"Over the years, others have seen the awful things you saw," said the hotel owner. "The pass is haunted. Too many died terrible deaths there for the spirits to be at rest."

Others may say the Englishwoman just had a bad dream that seemed real. It's only natural that the battle was on her mind as she fell asleep under the tree.

But those who live near the site of this bloody battlefield believe the land was witness to so much death and destruction that it can never erase the pain and violence.

Do images of past battles replay themselves again and again? The Englishwoman thought so. Do you?

Rosemary Brown

The nineteenth-century composer and pianist Franz Liszt first came to Rosemary Brown when she was seven years old. At the time of the visit, however, he had been dead for more than fifty years!

According to Rosemary, Liszt declared, "When you grow up, I will come back and give you music."

Years later, beginning in 1964, Rosemary, who lives in England, began communicating with a group of famous composers from the past. In addition to Liszt, they included Chopin, Beethoven, Bach, Brahms, Schumann, Schubert, Debussy, Grieg, and Rachmaninoff.

These men supposedly dictated musical compositions to Rosemary, who wrote them down in manuscript form. Then, with the help of her spirit friends, she played them on the piano.

"She's doing it herself," stated many nonbelievers. The music was analyzed by experts. Rosemary took psychological tests, intelligence tests, and musical tests. People investigated her background, her friends, her neighbors, and her musical training.

They found that Rosemary was a normal person of medium intelligence with a very limited musical background. She had taken some piano lessons, but stopped after a while. Poor since childhood, she had spent most of her life trying to make ends meet.

"Communicate with dead composers? Impossible!" declared one musician. "Perhaps she had advanced musical training, and then an episode of amnesia which made her forget," he suggested. Rosemary's family doctor stated that that was nonsense.

As a child she did have many psychic experiences. She often saw the spirits of dead people and realized at a young age that she had special powers and abilities.

In 1969, the British Broadcasting Corporation (BBC) did a documentary on Rosemary and her music. As a test, she sat at a piano, with BBC staff present, and waited for Liszt to put in an appearance.

In a matter of minutes, Liszt was there, dictating

a new piece. It was very difficult, with six sharps and different rhythms for the right and left hands. The completed manuscript was too hard for Rosemary herself to play. One of the BBC officials, who was an excellent pianist, was able to play it. He said, "Mrs. Brown, I think you've got something here!"

The piece was then analyzed by an expert on Franz Liszt. He stated that it was definitely characteristic of the great composer.

Rosemary has performed in a similar way with other composers who communicate with her. She sits at the piano and with great speed writes down what they dictate to her. Each completed piece is written in the exact style of that particular composer!

"Rosemary Brown is a gifted and talented musician," some experts say.

"Not true," replies Rosemary. "I am only the link to these great men. They dictate the music and I write it down."

How can it be proven that Rosemary is really in touch with the spirit world? For some, no amount of proof will ever be convincing. They are totally closed to the possibility.

But for other open-minded individuals, proof is possible. A Hungarian photographer named Tom Blau became a believer in 1970 when he was taking photos of Rosemary for the German magazine *Der Spiegel*. During the session, Rosemary admitted to the other journalists present that Liszt and her late mother were visible to her in the room.

Blau asked Liszt a question in German, a language Rosemary didn't understand. Rosemary said that Liszt nodded to her and answered, *"Ja,"* which means yes.

Then, according to Rosemary, Liszt said in English, "I'm going to fetch someone." He left the room. A few seconds later he returned. "He's back now," explained Rosemary to Blau and the other journalists, "and he's brought a woman with him." Rosemary went on to describe the woman in detail. "She's wearing a shawl and has very small feet," she added.

Blau's eyes widened. "You've just described my mother. I've always felt bad that I wasn't with her when she died," he said. "Now I feel better about it."

Later, Blau wrote to Rosemary: "I was moved and stirred by what occurred . . . You gave me a description so striking and convincing that I can't forget it."

How could Rosemary have known what Tom Blau's dead mother looked like? She had never met him before that day in 1970.

Did Rosemary really communicate with the famous composers of the past? Tom Blau thinks so.

Many believe Rosemary herself is the talent behind the music, not Liszt or Beethoven. Until there is more definite proof, the story of Rosemary Brown remains a strange, unsolved mystery.

A Mother's Warning

The American crew of the B-29 bomber was returning to their base in England during the last years of World War II. This long-range bomber was the largest and heaviest airplane of the war. Its payload of 20,000 pounds of bombs had been successfully dropped deep in the heart of enemy territory.

Most of the crew of twelve were asleep after the enemy raid. Only the pilot and copilot stayed awake to guide the B-29 home after the mission.

The night skies were clear of German fighter planes, but the pilots kept their eyes peeled for the enemy. If they were attacked, their thirteen machine guns and twenty-millimeter cannon could blow any speedy Messerschmitt fighter out of the sky.

A Mother's Warning

The young tail gunner was sound asleep in his revolving turret at the rear of the big bomber. In his dream, he suddenly saw his mother. She was standing on the wingtip of the airplane, dressed in a long, white robe that blew in the wind.

"Mom," the young corpsman said in his dream, quite astonished. "What are you doing here? You died three years ago. You're not even alive!"

"Son, wake up," she called to him. "Danger is very near. Wake up. You must wake up!"

The young flyer stirred in his sleep. His mother's voice echoed in his brain: "Wake up, wake up." Suddenly, the tail gunner awoke with a start.

"Mom?" he whispered. He realized the image of his mother had only been a dream. But just then he spotted a German fighter plane flying right above the B-29. The pilots would never have seen it from where they were seated.

"Wake up, everyone!" the tail gunner screamed over his microphone. "Bandit at twelve o'clock high! He appears to be all alone. Rise and shine, boys. Let's give the German on our tail a big Army Air Corps welcome!"

Although the speedy Messerschmitt Me 109 had two cannons and two machine guns, the lone German pilot wasn't prepared for the firepower that suddenly knocked him out of the sky.

"This is a message from my mother," said the tail gunner as he fired burst after burst at the enemy plane, which fell to the earth in flames. If his

mother hadn't appeared in his dream to warn and wake him, the B-29 would have been a sitting duck!

Are there limits to a mother's love? Did this woman come back from the dead to warn her son of danger? Or was it just a coincidence that he dreamed of her at that exact moment?

The young tail gunner was convinced that his mother saved his life and the lives of the crew. How would you explain it?

The Ghosts of
West Point

"The Thayer place is haunted," declared the major. "Strange things happen here."

The year was 1972, and Ed and Lorraine Warren had been invited to speak to the cadets at West Point. The Warrens were "demonologists," experts on the supernatural and the occult.

The major was giving them a tour of the U.S. Military Academy. Their first stop had been the white-painted brick Thayer residence.

"It's named for Colonel Sylvanus Thayer, who was West Point superintendent from 1817 to 1833," the major explained. "Our current superintendent lives here now."

"People have seen some unusual things at the house," he continued. "The beds are mysteriously turned down, and when they are made up, some invisible force turns them down again."

He then led the Warrens into the kitchen. "See that wet spot on the bread board? Whenever we dry it, it keeps coming back over and over again. It's been that way for months!" the major said.

"The superintendent and his wife have seen things at night and so have their guests. Doors slam and clothes are torn and ripped out of drawers," he added.

Lorraine could feel evidence of the supernatural at the Thayer house. There were troublesome spirits in the air.

In one of the rooms, Lorraine sat in a rocking chair and detected the presence of former President John F. Kennedy. She mentioned this to the major.

"JFK stayed in this room when he visited West Point," the major replied.

In the master bedroom, Lorraine felt the angry spirit of a strong woman who always got her way, "a jealous, possessive spirit who felt the house belonged to her and resented anybody else who lived in it," Lorraine declared.

When Lorraine told the major, he said that General Douglas MacArthur's wife had also lived in the Thayer house at one time. She ran the place with an iron hand, and the servants were afraid of her.

"That explains why the beds were always turned

down and why the clothes were tossed around," said the major.

But Lorraine sensed something else in the house. She believed some violent act had happened in or been connected with the house in some way.

Later that evening, after the Warrens had addressed the cadets, they were preparing to leave West Point. Lorraine glanced out the window and saw a ghostly figure of a man looking up at her. He wore an old-fashioned uniform from the past with no braids or insignia of any kind. Somehow he was able to communicate with Lorraine.

"He said his name was Greer and he was not free," Lorraine told one of the military aides accompanying them. But the name was not familiar to the young aide.

A week later Lorraine received a phone call. It was the aide from the academy.

"Mrs. Warren, I did some research on that man named Greer," he told her. "He attended West Point around the turn of the century and murdered another man. But he was cleared by a military court and absolved of blame, so why is his spirit so troubled?"

"We'll never really know the answer," explained Lorraine. "Perhaps he can't accept what happened and is still angry at himself."

Once the officials of West Point knew who all the ghosts were, they became less frightened and even more intrigued by their ghostly companions!

Dandy

The boy and his sister knew that their dog, Dandy, was devoted to them. He was a large and powerful retriever, trained as a gun dog for hunting. Sometimes Dandy acted so smart he almost seemed human.

Boy and dog went everywhere together. The boy was an expert duck and bird hunter and bicycled for miles around the beautiful English countryside to pursue his favorite sport.

Up at dawn, the boy and his dog spent their days traveling over hills and through swamps and grasslands. Dandy swam through the water and ran across the marshlands and fields. He loved to retrieve game for his beloved master.

Arriving home, Dandy would run and play with

the boy's sister or sometimes just nap at her feet. He felt peaceful and contented as the familiar, loving hand stroked his muscular back.

As the years went by, the boy and girl grew up and began spending less and less time with Dandy. But the dog was still devoted to them. Whenever the young man came home, the dog would accompany the family to the train station.

When the train came in, Dandy would run back and forth across the platform. As soon as he recognized his master, he would jump up on his hind legs and grab the hat off the young man's head. Then Dandy would trot home next to the car, hat in mouth, while the neighbors looked on with amusement.

One day, Dandy didn't come to the train station to meet the young man. When the master got home, he found that his devoted dog was very sick and couldn't walk.

Dandy was dying. For weeks during the winter, he had been retrieving sticks in the river. Then, night after night, he was mistakenly shut in the stable by the caretaker, soaking wet and without food.

The young man was heartbroken to see his ill dog. He held him close, whispering words of love and comfort to his pet. Dandy died that night in his master's arms.

At the same time, the man's sister was in Lon-

don, fast asleep in her room. Suddenly she awoke as a large dog jumped onto her bed.

The young woman switched on a small lamp next to the bed and saw Dandy. "Dandy boy," she said with delight. "What are you doing here?" She reached out to hug him and he licked her cheek. As she started to close her arms around the big dog, she suddenly found that she was hugging nothing but empty space!

"Well of course he can't be here," she said to herself. "I must be dreaming."

The young woman looked at her clock to see what time it was. She tried to get back to sleep but was too restless and worried. Something must be wrong at home, she thought to herself.

The next morning the young woman contacted her brother. She discovered that Dandy had died during the night at the very same time he had appeared in her room!

"I smelled Dandy and felt his tongue on my cheek," she told her brother.

Did the spirit of Dandy come to see his beloved mistress one last time? Or was it just her imagination?

"He came to say good-bye to me," she declared as tears filled her eyes, "and I will never forget him!"

A Feeling of Dread

"My dear, I don't feel very well," said Senator Lewis Linn of Missouri to his wife. "Probably an attack of indigestion. Will you go to the dinner party tonight and explain my absence to our host?"

"You don't look well, Lewis," replied Mrs. Linn. "I don't want to leave you alone tonight."

"Don't worry, dear," he explained. "General Jones will see you safely to the party, and he'll come back and stay with me during the evening. It's all been arranged."

The year was 1840, and the Linns lived in Washington, D.C., during the presidency of Martin Van Buren. At the party, Mrs. Linn sat next to General Macomb and opposite Senator Wright of New York, a close friend of her husband.

Mrs. Linn worried throughout the party. She tried to shake the feeling that something was dreadfully wrong at home. After all, her husband wasn't alone. In the event of an emergency, General Jones would notify her immediately.

As the night wore on, Mrs. Linn's uneasiness grew with each passing moment. Eventually she felt she must return home right away!

"Whatever is the matter?" asked Senator Wright when he saw how preoccupied she was.

Mrs. Linn explained her urgent feelings. Seeing her so pale and upset, Senator Wright and his wife took their friend home immediately.

At the door he said, "I'll call on you tomorrow and we'll have a good laugh about all this. I'm certain Lewis is fine!"

Mrs. Linn said good night, then went inside the house and spoke to the landlady.

"How is my husband feeling?" she asked.

"Very well, madam," the landlady replied. "He took a bath and is probably sound asleep by now. General Jones left a half-hour ago."

Mrs. Linn hurried upstairs to her husband's bedroom. When she opened the door, a blast of thick, dark smoke suddenly brought her to her knees. She scrambled up and rushed into the room.

The bed pillows were on fire! The air from the open door fanned the flames, and the fire burned brighter. She saw her husband lying on the bed, unconscious and at the mercy of the smoke and flames.

When Mrs. Linn ran to the bed to try to smother the blaze, her dress caught fire! As the flames spread over her clothes, she threw herself into the large tub that was still filled with water from her husband's bath. The flames were doused.

Pulling herself out of the tub, Mrs. Linn grabbed the burning pillows and plunged them into the bath water. Then, using what was left of her strength, she dragged her unconscious husband off the bed and screamed for help.

Later Dr. Sewell, the family physician, examined Senator Linn. "The senator is suffering from severe smoke inhalation," the doctor explained. "Three more minutes in that smoke-filled room and he would have died. You're lucky to have come at the exact moment you did!"

Mrs. Linn suffered burns on her arm. It took three months for her husband to fully recover from the accident. When Senator Wright heard what had happened, he was speechless.

How could Mrs. Linn have known that her husband would be in danger? She experienced a premonition, which is a warning of disaster.

Certain individuals have a special ability that extends beyond the normal five senses. This is called extrasensory perception, or ESP. Today, the knowledge of certain events before they actually

happen is called precognition. This phenomenon cannot be easily explained, even though it has been experienced by many people.

Was Mrs. Linn's feeling of danger a simple co-incidence, or was it real precognition?

The House on Plum Tree Lane

Harold Cameron was making a final inspection of the large mansion he had just rented. It was a twenty-minute drive outside of Philadelphia in the town of Wynne, Pennsylvania. The seventeen-room house dated back to revolutionary times and the grounds were beautifully landscaped.

It was the late 1940s and Harold needed a home for his family of seven. There was Harold's wife, Dorothy, his two college-age sons, Hal and Bob, ten-year-old Carrol, four-year-old Janet, and six-month-old Michael.

The Camerons had recently moved from the West Coast to the Philadelphia area. Harold had been chosen to open an office and warehouse there for the Aluminum Corporation of America.

The House on Plum Tree Lane

What a bargain, thought Harold as he examined his family's new home. They planned to move in the next day. "Three floors, four fireplaces, a circular staircase, servants' quarters, and all for only $300 a month!" he commented.

He walked down the stairway into the basement. "I'll check out the furnace," he said, looking around. "Everything else seems fine."

After he inspected the furnace, Harold walked back upstairs. As he headed for the front door, he heard the door to the library creak open, followed by the sound of footsteps. "Who is it?" he asked.

There was no answer. The afternoon sun had set, and it was dark inside the house.

"Is that you, Bob? Hal, are you there?" he called, thinking it might be his sons. "Answer me, please."

Harold lit a match. He saw the library door. "I'm sure that door was closed when I came in," he thought.

Suddenly the match flickered out. Again he heard footsteps. They seemed to go up the stairs right next to where Harold stood.

It sounds like a woman wearing floppy slippers, Harold thought as he lit another match. The sound was so close he felt he could have reached out and grabbed the person going upstairs.

All of a sudden the spot where Harold stood became icy cold. He grew frightened. "Who is it?" he called again. "Dorothy, is that you?"

Harold heard the footsteps on the second floor

and then on the third floor. Without waiting for an explanation, he bolted out the front door and found his family waiting for him in the car! None of them had been in the house!

By the time the Camerons moved in the next day, Harold was beginning to think he had imagined the whole thing. But he hadn't!

Two weeks later, Harold heard the footsteps again. Then Dorothy and the rest of the family heard them. The sounds seemed to come from the library.

Over the next several months, the Camerons heard footsteps on the drive outside the house. This time, however, they were heavy steps, crunching the gravel from the coach house to the main house and up to the front door. Then the sounds stopped.

"It's a man's footsteps, Dad," said Hal. "A big man. The ones inside the house are a woman's steps."

During the Camerons' stay in the mansion, they experienced a variety of ghostly phenomena. A terrible smell would come and go in a small part of the bedroom at night, and doorknobs would mysteriously turn without being touched.

After being thoroughly frightened in the beginning, the Camerons remained strong and eventually became accustomed to the ghostly sounds. They began to wonder what had happened to these restless spirits to make them haunt the house. They decided to try to find out.

The Camerons discovered an underground graveyard on the grounds near the house. They also found a secret room in the basement where runaway slaves were once hidden in the days before the Civil War.

When Harold hired Enoch, a very old man who used to work at the mansion as a young boy, the missing facts were finally pieced together.

A terrible crime had occurred in 1864. The fifteen-year-old daughter of the family that lived in the house at that time was assaulted and murdered by Ben, the coachman. He lured her out of the house by telling her that she needed to come see her injured pony in the barn. The girl's body was found in the nearby creek, and Ben was executed for his crime. The heavy footsteps outside the house were those of Ben's ghost!

The lady of the house couldn't cope with the loss of her only child. She was pained by anything that reminded her of her daughter, so she cleaned the library because her daughter had loved that room.

One day the mother walked up to the top floor and hung herself from the front window. It was this woman's ghostly footsteps the family heard inside the house!

After two years, the Camerons moved out of the house on Plum Tree Lane. They never came back. The new owners decided to remodel the large mansion and turn it into an apartment house. They never had trouble filling the units—all except for one. The room that had been the library has always stayed empty!

Nothing But Trouble

It may be hard to believe, but ghosts don't always haunt dark and gloomy houses located near cemeteries or built over ancient Indian burial grounds. Nor do they always die by violence or suffer a great injustice that must be righted before their spirits can rest in peace.

Take, for example, a modern colonial house, built in 1966 and located in a small town in Massachusetts. Strange incidents have occurred at this rather normal-looking two-story home. But most people hesitate to call the place haunted. Listen to the story of the family who lives in the house. Then you be the judge!

"Let your cat in already. It's cold outside," said a friend of the family one winter evening. "Can't you hear it clawing at the screen door?"

"I hear it," the owner replied.

"So do something. I think it's crawling up the screen!"

"I can't do anything," said the owner, "because the cats are already inside the house, and we don't even have a screen door!"

"Then what's making that noise?" asked the friend, thoroughly perplexed.

"You tell me," replied the owner.

Several days later, the owner's daughter and grandson were sitting in the kitchen. The daughter heard a car drive into the garage, a motor turn off, and a car door slam. Then someone walked through the garage and up the cellar steps, opened the door, and walked through the den and into the kitchen. The daughter turned around to say hello and saw . . . no one! When she went to the garage, it was empty.

Even today, the family hears strange knockings in the house, mysterious footsteps, and creaking doors. Often the lights, water faucets, and appliances are turned on and off. Can ghosts turn on radios or washing machines?

The owner thinks the strange incidents began when several very old family portraits, dating back to the 1840s, were hung in the living room.

Is there some connection between the pictures and the ghostly happenings? It's possible, but can ghosts from the midnineteenth century drive cars or operate blenders?

The owner's family isn't afraid. If strange things happen, one would go outside and sit on the porch until other people come home. But they do feel a bit uneasy. After all, these things keep happening and there's no logical explanation for them.

Do ghosts really haunt this house, or is it the overactive imagination of the human inhabitants? Are there really troublesome spirits moving about, or just someone's forgetfulness in turning off lights and radios?

D. D. Home

It was December 1868, and the famous medium
D. D. Home was giving a séance. Home was
known for his power to communicate with the
dead. As a physical medium, his typical séance included objects that moved, musical instruments
that played by themselves, and other visible phenomena.

Those present at the séance were the Master of
Lindsay, Viscount Adare, and Captain Charles
Wynne. They were seated around the table as
Home went into a trance.

"Do not be afraid," Home told the three men.
"Do not leave your seats."

The medium then got up and walked into the
next room, and the men heard a window open.

Within seconds, Home appeared, standing upright, *outside* the window of the room in which the three men sat. He then opened the window and glided in, feet first.

What is especially remarkable about this is that the windows were several stories off the ground! There was a very narrow ledge under the windows, but it was not wide enough to stand on. Therefore, Home must have *floated* through the air to get from one window to the next! All three witnesses testified that this was exactly what took place.

They shouldn't have been surprised, since Home was famous for spectacular phenomena. During a trance, he often levitated, rising up off the ground and floating to the ceiling with his arms above his head. Sometimes he even grew five or six inches taller during a séance while under spiritual control!

Home usually gave sittings in the bright light of day because he had nothing to hide. Participants often clearly saw strange moving lights, phantom hands that melted away, and tables that moved or rose in the air. Once Home placed his face into the burning coals of a fireplace without injury.

Throughout his career, Home was subjected to thorough investigation and testing. Many mediums at that time used trickery and fraud to deceive people. Never once was Home found to have "cheated" during a sitting!

During a séance, an investigator reported that "the table was seen to rise completely from the

floor and floated about in the air for several seconds." One man actually sat on top of the table, and it still moved around!

Throughout Home's life, nonbelievers attempted to come up with explanations as to how he accomplished such incredible feats at his séances. Some say he hypnotized participants into believing these amazing things happened. Others say the séance participants were Home's followers, who would never doubt the ability of their leader and might have imagined or exaggerated what actually took place. But no matter how hard they tried, these nonbelievers could find no evidence of trickery.

Were the spirits of the dead responsible for Home's spectacular séances? There is no question that he possessed amazing powers that have, so far, been unequaled and remain unexplained.

Borley Rectory

What ghostly phenomena have *not* taken place at Borley Rectory? The answer is very few.

Since the 1860s, scores of people have reported mysterious and unexplained occurrences at Borley Rectory, near Sudbury in Suffolk, England. (A rectory is the house in which a minister lives.)

There have been sounds of whispering, horses galloping, church music, bells ringing, footsteps, knocking, bumps, thuds, wailing, rustling, crashing, and windows breaking.

People have seen the ghosts of a nun, a headless man, a figure in gray, a girl in white, a coach drawn by horses, and other shadowy figures. There have been wall writings, lighted windows, swinging blinds, cold spots, good and bad odors, and unexplained footprints.

It seems that Borley Rectory has been the center of supernatural disturbances for some time. To discover why, a look back at the history of the area is necessary.

Records show that a monastery existed in Borley as early as the thirteenth century. One story of that time that may be true is told of a monk from the monastery who fell in love with a local nun. The two planned to run away together, but they were caught and punished. The monk was hanged and, according to legend, a brick wall was built to seal the nun, alive, in the cellar.

In the years that followed, residents reported seeing the ghost of a nun near the monastery. But it wasn't until 1863, when the Reverend Henry Bull built a new rectory on the exact site, that incidents began to happen more frequently.

A nursemaid reported hearing ghostly footsteps. The Bull daughters saw the nun several times, and the cook saw a strange figure in the garden who suddenly disappeared.

Henry's son, the Reverend Harry Bull, and his family also saw the ghost of the nun. Their servants claimed to have seen a ghost coach with ghost horses.

The Cooper family, who lived in the cottage near the rectory, also saw the coach and horses, heard strange noises, and were terrified by a black shape in their bedroom.

After Harry Bull died in 1927, the Reverend Smith moved into the rectory with his family. He called in psychic Harry Price to investigate. When Price arrived at the rectory, he was met with showers of stones and other unusual activity. The Smith family couldn't cope with the ghosts and moved out, but Price remained to study the phenomena.

In 1930, Reverend Foyster and his family moved in, and more violent incidents were recorded. On several occasions, Foyster was pelted with stones, and his wife was thrown from her bed. Doors locked, music played, and bottles smashed, all seemingly on their own. After five difficult years, the Foysters, too, left the rectory.

In 1937, Harry Price rented it for a year. He recruited a random cross-section of people to act as impartial observers of the ghostly phenomena. Incidents were often witnessed by several people at a time and records were kept. Eventually Price gathered enough material to write two books about the Borley Rectory.

Several new stories emerged about the identity of the mysterious nun. One stated that Henry Waldegrave, whose family had owned the land long ago, married a French woman who was a former nun and later murdered her in the rectory. Another said the nun was Arabella Waldegrave, who was a spy against the British Commonwealth, and that she, too, was murdered at Borley.

A mysterious fire in 1939 burned the rectory to the ground. In 1943, Harry Price and several others dug through the ruins and found a jawbone of a woman and part of a human skull. Could this have been the remains of the unhappy nun whose ghost haunted the area? Price laid the bones to rest in a Christian burial.

The strange incidents continued at Borley even after the fire. Harry Price was still involved in studying the mysterious events when he died in 1949. Years after his death, some accused Price of staging many of the ghostly incidents. Yet strange happenings occurred and were reported by numerous people before *and* after Harry Price ever became involved.

Were the noises people heard just the scratchings of rats and birds in the rectory attic? Did mischievous village boys throw stones and bottles at the house, causing loud thuds and crashing sounds? Were the ghostly figures just hallucinations or real people who were mistakenly identified?

Or is the ground around Borley a haunted place of power that allows certain psychically gifted people to see the ghosts? For example, in one incident a man clearly saw the spirit of a woman in a long white gown, while his companion only heard the rustle of trees and bushes.

Photographers have noticed that after developing their photos of the churchyard at Borley, strange, unexplained shapes and faces appear in them. Yet they didn't see these images when they took the pictures!

Whatever the explanation, Borley Church and the site of the rectory still make many people very uneasy. Some people say it still looks and feels haunted, but most visitors don't stay long enough to find out!

The Divining Dowser

A bacon-curing plant in Waterford, Ireland, needed a large supply of water to process its bacon. The owners decided to dig a well on their property to tap into a natural water source below.

Several holes were dug by engineers, but none was successful in reaching water. One seven-inch hole, which was more than 1,000 feet deep, yielded no water at all!

The manager finally sent for a water diviner named John Mullins, who practiced the ancient art of dowsing. Mullins used a forked stick made of hazelwood about twelve or fifteen inches long. He held each end between his second and third fingers. He then walked around the property, holding the stick horizontally in front of him. Almost immediately, the stick bent slightly by itself.

"Mark that spot," instructed Mullins to the plant manager.

As Mullins moved on, several other places were marked. A few clerks from the plant watched Mullins carefully. Some even held on to the stick, placing their hands over his. "The stick is moving by itself," said the clerks in amazement. "His hands are completely still!" At one spot in particular, the stick lifted itself up and twisted around until it broke!

"There's water here," Mullins declared. "It's not more than eighty feet down. Try this place first."

A hole was dug. At about 75 feet, water was discovered. When the well was completed, it pumped about 2,000 gallons per hour, much to the delight of the plant owners.

How could Mullins have located the exact spot at which the water supply could be obtained? How did he correctly predict the depth of the water? And finally, how did the dowser succeed where engineers and geologists failed?

Dowsing may have existed as early as prehistoric man. The practice is still widespread and very successful today. The big question is, how and why does it work?

. Some believe a force, such as vibrations, electromagnetic waves, or even radiation is emitted from the water. This force then affects the stick or even,

perhaps, the mind of the dowser. Others say that dowsing is a psychic experience. The dowser's muscles respond to extrasensory stimulation, causing the stick to move. Many dowsers feel strange or even sick when the rod moves in their hands. Some have described it as "a tingling or electric shock," "a trembling," or "a spasm."

Dowsers have been successful in finding hidden or missing objects as well as underground water. Some even use metal rods instead of a forked dowsing stick. Others use nothing at all. They just seem to know where the water or object is located.

No one knows exactly how or why dowsing is successful. What's important is that it seems to work!

Rajah

"I may not be back this afternoon," eighteen-year-old Ruth Rockwell announced to her sister-in-law. Ruth was a moody girl and very much obsessed with death. She believed in reincarnation. She felt that after people died they were reborn into a new body or new form of life.

"Good-bye, Rajah," said Ruth to the large and gentle Great Dane who stood quietly as he watched her leave. She patted his head and walked out the door. '

"What a strange young woman!" thought Mrs. Rockwell as she went about her morning chores. It was November 11, 1930. Ruth had been staying with them for several months.

The Rockwells lived on a small farm in New

York's Westchester County. Donald, Ruth's brother, took the train each morning to his job in Manhattan.

At three o'clock that afternoon, Mrs. Rockwell was sitting in the living room when Rajah suddenly ran upstairs. He came back down with a pillow in his mouth and placed it at the astonished woman's feet.

"How thoughtful, Rajah! A cushion for my feet!" she exclaimed with a chuckle. "What are you up to?"

Rajah raced back upstairs and returned carrying a coat in his mouth. He laid it on top of the pillow.

"Why, that's Ruth's coat," said Mrs. Rockwell.

Again, the dog ran back upstairs and this time came down with one of Ruth's hats.

The Great Dane then lay down, put his head on the pillow, hat, and coat, and began whining and whimpering.

"Poor boy," said Mrs. Rockwell. "What are you upset about? Did Ruth forget her hat and coat? And is that her pillow, too?"

Sure enough, Rajah had taken the pillow from Ruth's bed. After a few minutes, Mrs. Rockwell returned the items to their proper places. She was still thinking about the dog's odd behavior when the phone rang a half-hour later. It was the police.

"Mrs. Rockwell," the officer said. "I'm sorry to have to inform you that your sister-in-law, Ruth Rockwell, is dead."

Mrs. Rockwell was shocked. The officer related that Ruth had been a passenger on a small private plane that flew people on short sightseeing trips over Long Island. The pilot recalled that she had been very nervous on the flight and seemed to be praying.

"But a lot of people are nervous if it's their first plane ride," the pilot declared. "I felt the airplane sway a bit, and when I looked around she was gone. It was as if she had disappeared into thin air. It's an awful tragedy."

Ruth had jumped out of the plane and was killed. It was the first time a woman had ever committed suicide in such a way.

When the Rockwells returned home that night from the police station, weary and numb with grief, Mrs. Rockwell told her husband about Rajah's strange behavior.

"What time did you say this happened?" he asked.

"About three o'clock," replied his wife.

"That's almost the exact time Ruth was killed," he declared. "It's almost as if Rajah knew what had happened."

Suddenly the Great Dane, who had been lying next to their bed, jumped up, ran to the window, and started barking furiously. Then he rushed back, put his paws on Mrs. Rockwell's knees, and growled in the direction of the street. Again Rajah ran to the window, snarling and baring his teeth.

The hair on his neck and back stood up as he barked and growled.

Mr. Rockwell looked out the window. "No one's out there, boy," he said, trying to calm the usually gentle dog.

"You mean, no one you can see!" said his wife nervously. It was nine o'clock.

Later the Rockwells discovered a note written by Ruth before her suicide. It said, "If there is a spirit world, I will attempt to communicate with someone in the family at nine o'clock."

Did Rajah see the ghost of Ruth? Can dogs instinctively know things that people don't? Do they have an extra sense that allows them to see what humans are unable to?

After a time, things returned to normal in the Rockwell home. The Great Dane often sat next to Ruth's favorite chair, resting his head on its arm as if he was waiting to be stroked by someone who wasn't there.

Ghost Toys

"Can you help me, please?" the woman customer asked the salesclerk at a Toys " " Us store in Sunnyvale, California. "This talking doll must be defective. It hasn't said a word, and my daughter is very disappointed."

"Let me try it, ma'am," said the clerk. She tilted the doll, pressed its stomach, and turned it upside down. The toy was stubbornly silent.

"Why don't you pick out another one and I'll send this one back to the manufacturer," she said, putting the doll into its box.

"Thank you, dear," smiled the woman. She turned and walked away down the nearest aisle.

"Another satisfied customer," thought the salesclerk to herself. She closed the lid of the box and was about to shelve it when she suddenly heard sounds. The clerk put her ear to the box.

"Mama, Mama, Mama," the doll repeated over and over again. After a period of silence, the doll talked again. Puzzled, the clerk took the toy to the stockroom. There, the doll actually started to make crying sounds!

"Very strange," thought the clerk later as she sat alone in the employee lounge. "The voice mechanism must be jammed or something."

Suddenly the bulletin board on the wall started to move back and forth.

"Anybody here?" said the clerk nervously. She looked around and found she was still alone.

As she stared at the bulletin board, a stack of papers piled on top of the nearby refrigerator floated slowly to the floor, one sheet at a time.

"Okay, that's it. Let me out of here!" she declared out loud. The frightened clerk had to stop herself from breaking into a run as she left the lounge.

Other employees at this Toys " " Us have experienced unexplained and mysterious incidents. One manager had just locked up the store for the night when he heard a loud banging inside the building. Could someone have been locked inside accidentally? He went back in, but the building was empty. Shrugging his shoulders, the manager locked the doors once more. As he walked to his car, the loud banging started up again. This happened several more times before the man simply ignored the banging and went home.

Another clerk heard her name called over and over again by a mysterious voice and felt invisible fingers in her hair. One customer complained that the water faucets in the ladies' room were turning on and off by themselves. Merchandise moved during the night, shelves fell over, and lights turned on and off without explanation.

As the incidents continued, more and more employees began to believe the store was haunted. Several investigated the history of the area in which the store was built, hoping to find clues to identify the ghost or ghosts.

At first some workers believed the ghost of Martin Murphy, the founder of Sunnyvale, haunted the toy store. But after psychic Sylvia Brown spent a night in the store, most believed the restless spirit was that of a preacher named Yon Johnson.

Yon had lived with a family whose farm was on the site of the toy store at the turn of the century. He loved a girl named Elizabeth, who may have been the daughter of Martin Murphy. She eventually married someone else, but Yon never stopped loving her and remained a bachelor all his life.

Sylvia Brown had visions of Yon walking through the store, which he still saw as the farm on which he lived. She saw him pumping water from a spring, which employees later discovered had once been located right under the toy store.

Do the mysterious happenings in Sunnyvale have logical but overlooked explanations? Is the ghost of restless and lovesick Yon still searching for his lost love? Or do the employees of the toy store have overactive imaginations?

Perhaps we will never know the answer. But now, whenever something strange and unexplained happens at this particular toy store, the employees just say, "Yonny's at it again!"

Fire!

The dinner party had just begun in Göteborg, Sweden. The famous scientist and psychic Emanuel Swedenborg was among sixteen guests on the evening of July 19, 1759.

Swedenborg had studied engineering and written books about the animal kingdom, the human brain, and psychology. Since 1747, however, he had devoted himself only to matters of a spiritual nature, such as psychic visions and communication with the spirit world.

Suddenly, just after dinner had been served, Swedenborg stood up and walked quickly out of the house without speaking to anyone.

When the host of the party came into the room, he noticed that Swedenborg was missing. "Where did the doctor go? He was here only a minute ago," the host asked one of the guests.

"He stepped outside," replied the woman. "But he had the strangest expression on his face."

Swedenborg soon returned. "Here he is now! Emanuel, come sit down. You look ill and you're trembling," the host exclaimed.

"Whatever is wrong?" asked the concerned woman.

Swedenborg began to speak slowly. "I see a fire, a horrible blaze in Stockholm. It's out of control, racing through the city."

"But that's three hundred miles from here!" whispered the woman, somewhat astonished.

For several hours, Swedenborg described the details of the fire as it was occurring. "It has already destroyed my friend's home, and now it's threatening my own house," he said sadly.

The guests were startled, but the party continued. Finally, at approximately 8 P.M., Swedenborg made an announcement. "The fire is out. It has been stopped just three doors from my home!"

The next day, everyone wondered if there really had been a fire. Was Swedenborg's vision accurate? Was it all a trick? There was no telegraph or radio at that time, so it was impossible to find out the truth immediately.

Two days after the dinner party, a courier arrived from Stockholm with news. He confirmed that there had been a devastating fire in the Swedish city. As details of the disaster emerged, they matched everything Swedenborg had described. Most amazing was the fact that the blaze had indeed been halted only three houses from Swedenborg's residence, just as he had stated!

This incident of clairvoyance (which means to become aware of events or objects without the use of the usual five senses) was verified by numerous witnesses at the dinner party. Although the case was widely investigated, no reason or explanation for Swedenborg's vision could be given, other than extrasensory perception.

Was it a clear case of clairvoyance? If not, how could Swedenborg have known so many details about a fire that happened three hundred miles away?

Edgar Cayce

In 1904, Edgar Cayce (pronounced *KAY*-cee), a salesman in a bookstore in Bowling Green, Kentucky, lay down on an operating table at the local doctor's office. He crossed his hands over his stomach, shut his eyes, and breathed deeply a few times.

Observing Cayce in the room were several well-known doctors from Bowling Green, along with a college professor. Within minutes, Cayce was in a deep sleep and his eyelids began to flicker. One of the physicians walked over to the table.

"Mr. Cayce," he said, "I'm presently treating a six-year-old boy named Jonathan Brooks. You don't know him. He lives on South Main Street in Bowling Green and is sick in bed right now. Will you please describe his physical condition for me?"

After a few seconds, Cayce, still sleeping in a trancelike state, replied, "Yes, we have the body. There's excessive fluid in the right lung, and no air can be inhaled into the lung. The left lung was once involved but is almost normal now. There's also an inflammation in the stomach."

"Thank you, Mr. Cayce," said the doctor. Turning to the others in the room, the physician declared, "Gentlemen, Mr. Cayce's diagnosis is perfectly correct! We will continue this demonstration with additional test cases, all of whom are total strangers to Mr. Cayce."

The sleeping man went on to diagnose other patients correctly and, in some cases, prescribed particular medicine or treatment. While in his trance, he was able to pinpoint abnormalities and diseases. Then he would suggest a remedy without ever seeing or examining the actual patient!

This extraordinary man, with no background or training in medicine or surgery, gave thousands of medically correct "readings" throughout his life, many over long distances.

He was called a healer, a clairvoyant, a seer, and a psychic, sensitive to supernatural and extrasensory forces. But Edgar Cayce, a deeply religious man, believed he simply had a gift from God.

Born on March 18, 1877, Cayce was a farm boy who showed an early interest in religion and the Bible. At age fifteen, he was hit on the head by a baseball and went into a coma. During the coma, he spoke clearly to his parents, prescribing what they should do to make him well. This was his first reading.

During another illness when he was twenty-three, Cayce lost his voice for ten months. When all medical help failed, a hypnotist named Al C. Layne put him into a trance in a last-ditch effort to cure him. Under hypnosis, Cayce began talking normally in a full, steady voice. He explained that there was a partial paralysis of the vocal cords and then prescribed his own cure. The hypnotist realized the potential of Cayce's power. The readings continued and Cayce's reputation grew.

Cayce cured his wife's tuberculosis and his son's partial blindness. He gave correct medical readings for patients hundreds of miles away. All he needed were their names and exact locations.

He used his power in other areas, too. He sometimes helped the police solve difficult crimes. In one case, Cayce gave the exact location of a murder weapon. The police wanted to arrest him as the murderer because they were convinced that only the criminal would know such details!

Later in his life, Cayce gave "life readings" in which he told people about their past lives (reincarnation). Cayce himself believed he had been, in previous lives, an Egyptian high priest named Ra Ta, an English soldier in colonial times named John Bainbridge, and a Persian warrior named Uhjltd. He claimed he had also been a Greek named Xenon and a follower of Jesus named Lucius.

Edgar Cayce died on January 3, 1945. At the time of his death, he was receiving four to five hundred letters daily asking for help. To fulfill this demand, Cayce pushed himself to give eight readings a day.

He was called the "most gifted psychic of our time." Cayce once said about his powers, "I don't do anything you can't do."

Disaster at Sea

It was a cold April evening. The mid-Atlantic Ocean was covered in thick fog as a giant ocean liner sped along. The huge ship was traveling at more than twenty knots—too fast for such poor weather conditions. Almost 800 feet long, the ship carried only twenty-four lifeboats, certainly not enough for the 3,000 passengers aboard.

Dead ahead and partially obscured by the fog lay a giant iceberg. Most of the large mass of ice was hidden below the surface of the water. Unaware of the danger, the crew of the luxury liner continued on a collision course with the iceberg.

Does this scene sound familiar? Could this be a description of the *Titanic* disaster of April 14, 1912? Guess again! It is a description of the fictional ship *Titan* from a novel called *Futility* by Morgan Robertson. The amazing thing is that this novel was written in 1898, fourteen years *before* the *Titanic*'s first and final voyage!

There are many similarities between the fictitious novel and the actual event. To begin with, the names of the two ships are nearly identical. Both were described as the largest and fastest vessels afloat—"unsinkable" and "indestructible." Each ship had three propellers and two masts, and carried the same number of passengers.

Did the author of *Futility* have a prophetic vision of what was to happen years in the future? Or was the similarity of his fictional account just a coincidence?

Warnings of impending disaster aboard luxury liners occurred as early as the 1880s. A journalist named W. T. Stead warned that ships didn't carry enough lifeboats for their crews and passengers. In 1892, Stead wrote a fictional account of an ocean liner's colliding with an iceberg in the Atlantic. In the story, many died in the icy waters after the ship sank.

This same journalist was aboard the *Titanic* on April 10, 1912, when it sailed from Southampton, England. Stead was among the more than fifteen hundred victims who died in the freezing waters of the Atlantic when the great liner went down. Ironically, despite his warnings about the lack of lifeboats, he became a victim himself.

Many people had premonitions about the *Titanic* disaster. An engineer turned down a job in the *Titanic*'s engine room because he felt something terrible would happen. Others felt superstitious about sailing on the maiden voyage of any ship. The wealthy banker J. Pierpont Morgan was one of those who canceled his sailing plans for this reason. A man had a dream that the *Titanic* was shipwrecked, so he booked passage on another ship. One woman, watching the giant liner steam out to sea, screamed to her husband, "It's going to sink! Do something! Save them!"

On April 14, four days after the *Titanic* set out to sea, the ocean was covered in fog. The ship sped along at 22½ knots. There had been warnings of icebergs, but the crew was not worried. After all, the *Titanic* was "unsinkable"!

At 11:40 P.M., the luxury ship hit the iceberg below the waterline, tearing open its hull. Most passengers felt only a small shudder. Five compartments flooded immediately and the rest filled gradually. Seawater poured in and the ship slowly began sinking.

Over two thousand people were aboard, but there were only twenty lifeboats. About 700 survived, even though many of the lifeboats weren't even close to being filled to capacity before they were lowered into the water.

Hundreds froze or drowned in the water, screaming for help that never came. A large num-

ber stayed on board as the *Titanic* rose straight up out of the water, then sank quickly and quietly to the depths of the ocean.

Why were there so many premonitions and warnings of the *Titanic* disaster? Were they true cases of precognition, clairvoyance relating to the future?

Huge icebergs, bad weather, speedy ocean liners, and the lack of lifeboats were a dangerous combination. Was a horrible accident bound to happen eventually?

Some good did come out of this disaster. The sinking of the *Titanic* resulted in the passage of many new safety rules and regulations for ocean-going ships. With this knowledge and awareness, many such disasters at sea were avoided in the future.

The Haunted Family

It was 1973 when the Smurl family moved into the house in West Pittston, Pennsylvania. Soon afterward, their troubles began.

Small things happened at first. An unexplained grease stain on the carpet kept coming back even after repeated cleanings. One night, the TV set burst into flames. Mysterious scratches appeared on the sink and tub after the bathroom was remodeled. The toilet flushed by itself. The radio played when it wasn't even plugged in. Drawers opened and closed in the bedrooms.

Then, more frightening things began to happen.

"Janet," whispered the soft, strange voice. Janet Smurl was alone in the basement doing laundry. At least she thought she was alone.

"Janet," whispered the voice again.

She whirled around but saw no one. Thoroughly shaken, she backed up the stairs slowly and slammed the door to the basement. Had she imagined a voice calling to her?

Several days passed. Janet was in the kitchen ironing. She looked up and saw a black form floating toward her. As it moved closer, she smelled a strange odor and felt a cold chill. The shape glided into the living room and vanished.

One evening, something grabbed Janet's leg and tried to pull her off the bed. Her husband, Jack, had to tug with all his strength to keep her from being pulled away.

At night the family regularly heard banging and pounding inside the walls of the house. The family dog was picked up by an unseen force and thrown against the kitchen door. One of the Smurl's four daughters was struck by a heavy overhead light that had somehow torn itself out of the ceiling.

The Smurls, who were Roman Catholic, asked two priests to bless their house. For several days after each blessing, the house was quiet. But each time the trouble started up again.

Demonologists Ed and Lorraine Warren were invited to visit. Using Lorraine's powers as a medium, they determined that three spirits and a demon haunted the house.

One spirit was an elderly woman who was found to be confused and harmless. A younger female spirit turned out to be insane and violent. The third spirit was a man who seemed to be controlled by the demon, who Lorraine said was "here to create chaos and destroy the family!"

According to Ed Warren, the demon and spirits had always been in the house but had been quiet until now. They became active by drawing on the energy of the Smurls' teenage daughters.

Armed with holy water blessed by the church, the Smurls continued to resist the demon, who in turn became more violent. Jack was physically attacked and bitten in the shower. The rapping and scratching noises continued inside the walls. Terrible odors and drastic drops in temperature occurred without warning.

The Warrens brought in Father Robert McKenna of Connecticut who performed two separate exorcisms. An exorcism is a church ritual to cast out demons. Both were unsuccessful, and the haunting continued.

The Smurls' sixteen-year-old daughter was attacked in the shower. A younger daughter was mysteriously lifted off her bed and suspended in midair. Jack was thrown to the floor. Another daughter was picked up and hurled out of bed during the night. The noises went on and on.

When Jack and Janet spent a weekend away from their home, the demon followed them to their motel and continued to attack them. Later, when

the family went on a camping trip, the demon again followed them.

Would they ever be free?

There were additional attacks on the family, even more vicious and brutal than before. The Smurls retaliated by sprinkling holy water and saying prayers.

In the hope that they could get more help, the family went public, describing their problems on television and in newspapers and magazines. Scores of curious people drove by their home and camped-out on their lawn. Neighbors and friends were very supportive. The Smurls found out that six other homes on their block were experiencing rapping noises, bad odors, and screaming sounds.

A prayer meeting was organized. Fifty women and twenty men filled the Smurl home, each of them holding a candle as they all prayed together.

Jack and Janet had hoped to have several priests participate in a mass exorcism at the house, but the diocese of the Catholic Church declined to participate. Priests were sent to stay overnight at the Smurl house, but they heard and saw nothing unusual. Therefore, the church felt there was no proof of a haunting.

Father McKenna returned and performed a third exorcism. This time, friends and relatives held daily prayer vigils during and after the ritual. Within days, the scent of roses filled the Smurl home!

Weeks went by without incident. Months passed, and the Smurls enjoyed the peace and quiet of a normal family. But it didn't last.

In December 1986, the haunting began again. The following year, the Smurl family moved to another town in Pennsylvania.

Will the demon follow them there? Will they ever be really free again? Only time will tell. In the meantime, their continued faith and love for one another helps the family to cope with whatever each new day brings.

The Tower of London

The night guard at the Tower of London stood frozen and paralyzed with fear. This can't be happening, he thought to himself. I must be dreaming!

There, in plain sight of the guard, was a woman dressed in sixteenth-century clothing, accompanied by a group of men and women in similar dress. They walked the grounds of the Tower Green.

As the guard watched in horror, he realized that something was very wrong. He studied the faces of the strange procession, and then he suddenly understood, just before he fainted, what was so peculiar about the first woman.

"She has no head!" he exclaimed, and then he blacked out.

When you are a guard on the night shift at the

Tower of London, seeing ghosts is not that uncommon. The tower has been called one of the world's bloodiest historic sites! Used mainly as a prison and place of execution, hundreds of people were hanged and beheaded in the tower. Kings, queens, counts, and countesses were among those who met their deaths within the tower walls. Their ghosts reportedly still haunt the grounds.

Many towers, buildings, and yards make up the eighteen acres known as the Tower of London. Today, it is a popular tourist attraction where the crown jewels are kept.

The headless noblewoman the guard saw was very likely the ghost of Anne Boleyn, the second wife of King Henry VIII. She has been said to appear with or without her head, leading a group of lords and ladies of the court. Anne was beheaded on the Tower Green in 1536 because she couldn't bear King Henry a son. But Anne had the last laugh on Henry. Her daughter, Elizabeth I, became Queen of England and reigned for forty-five years!

In those days, most executions were performed with an ax to the neck. Sometimes several blows were needed to cut off the unfortunate victim's head. Anne was afraid of the ax and had a swordsman from France brought in to behead her in a single stroke.

Over the years, other tower guards have reported seeing ghosts. One terrified sentry saw a

stretcher carried by two men. On the stretcher was a body with its head tucked under one arm.

The ghosts of the twelve-year-old boy-king, Edward V, and his younger brother, Richard, are reported to have appeared in the Bloody Tower. They were imprisoned in the tower in the late fifteenth century and may have been murdered there.

Another tower ghost is the seventy-year-old Countess of Salisbury, who was ordered beheaded by Henry VIII in 1541. She refused to bend over the chopping block, and the executioner chased her around the Tower Green with his ax!

The ghost of Lady Jane Grey was seen by two tower guards in 1957 on the roof of the Salt Tower. First, Lady Jane watched as her husband was executed. Then she herself was beheaded at the age of fifteen.

If ghosts are the spirits of restless and unhappy people, the Tower of London, with its bloody history, has reason to have countless numbers of them roaming around.

The Gray Ghost

"No sign of the gray ghost," said the director quietly to the producer of a lavish American musical. The two men were rehearsing the show at the Theatre Royal in London, England.

"Did I hear you say 'ghost'?" asked the young actress who had a supporting role in the show.

The director took the young woman aside. "You may not believe this, but the theater is haunted," he said.

The young woman's eyes widened.

"Before you begin to think I'm crazy," explained the director, "let me assure you that the gray ghost—some call him the gray man—has been seen by hundreds of people for more than a hundred years."

"I didn't know this place was that old," declared the young woman.

"This building was built in 1812," the director continued. "Three previous buildings on this site were either destroyed by fire or torn down."

The famous Theatre Royal has been the site of many hit musicals such as *Hello Dolly!*, *Oklahoma*, and *South Pacific*. The ghost that haunts this theater is unlike other spirits, however. He doesn't intentionally scare or terrorize anyone, nor does he make any sounds. He simply walks around the theater.

"People say he comes out of the wall on the upper circle level, where we are now, and walks to the other side of the theater," the director continued. "The ghost only appears in the daytime, and sometimes when there's a matinee. In fact, some members of the audience have actually seen him during a performance," he added.

"Who was he and why is he haunting the theater?" asked the young actress.

"No one really knows," the director answered. "But in 1848, a tiny room was discovered bricked-up inside the walls of the theater. Inside the room was a skeleton with a dagger in its ribs."

"That explains it!" she exclaimed. "Maybe the gray ghost is the unhappy spirit of the man who was murdered so many years ago. The murderer obviously hid the body."

"The bones were given a proper burial in a cemetery, but the ghost keeps appearing in the theater," added the director.

"I don't want to sound offensive or anything," said the actress, "but why are you so interested in this ghost? It sounds as if you're actually waiting for him to appear."

"This may sound strange to you, but if the ghost is seen before a new show starts, it's considered good luck," the director explained. "In the past, the gray ghost has appeared before hit shows, but he was nowhere to be seen at all the flops."

The young actress nodded. "Now I understand. You want him to come before the curtain goes up tonight, so the musical will be a hit!"

"Let me put it this way," the director said, smiling. "The show is great. The tunes are great. The cast is great. I'm convinced it will be a hit. But it would be nice if the gray ghost put in an appearance—as insurance, of course."

"So what does he look like?" the woman questioned.

"He wears a long, dark gray cape over a coat with ruffled sleeves," the director explained. "He carries a sword and wears riding boots."

The actress's eyes grew wide again. "Does he wear a big, dark hat over a powdered gray wig?"

"Why, yes, but how did you know?" the director asked, puzzled. Then, following her gaze, he turned slowly and looked behind him.

The director and actress stared openmouthed at

the sight of the gray ghost across the room, some thirty-five feet away. Obviously a gentleman, he moved silently across the room, keeping his distance. Then he passed through the door and out of sight.

The man and woman slowly turned to look at each other. "You'd better close your mouth before a fly settles in it. We have just seen the gray ghost!" the director said, grinning from ear to ear. "Sweetheart, we have a hit!"

He reached over, gave the actress a bear hug, and ran off. "I've got to tell the producer!"

The young actress sat down and took a deep breath. "Tonight is opening night and I have just seen a ghost! Oh, well," she shrugged. "That's show business."

The Bell Witch

At first there were unusual noises at the Bell House in Robertson County, Tennessee—knocking, scraping, clawing, and flapping sounds. Then it got much worse for John Bell, his wife, Lucy, and their nine children.

The year was 1817. A mischievous ghost, called a poltergeist, began to pull sheets and blankets off the beds and make gulping, choking, and strangling sounds. Then it began to throw stones and turn chairs upside down. The disturbances seemed to focus around twelve-year-old Betsy Bell.

One night the poltergeist yanked the hair of two of the children so hard that they began to scream in pain. Betsy was scratched and slapped across the face by an unseen hand. Sometimes visitors to the house even received slaps!

The Bell Witch

The poltergeist began making whistling sounds, which gradually developed into a low gasping. Some believe that Betsy unknowingly provided the energy for the disturbances.

The voice identified itself as a witch named Old Kate Batts. It had several other personalities, including an Indian and a man.

"I am a spirit who was once very happy," declared the witch, "but I have been disturbed and now am unhappy."

The witch eventually turned her focus to John Bell, declaring she would torment and kill him! Soon afterward, Bell's tongue swelled and he couldn't eat for days at a time. The witch cursed at him and used bad language.

The spirit yanked off the man's shoes. She hit him in the face so hard he went into convulsions. The witch shrieked with laughter at his agony. After three years of this abuse, Bell became physically ill and depressed.

The witch was still cruel to young Betsy, but she could also be nice. On Betsy's birthday, a basket of oranges and bananas appeared out of thin air as a gift to the girl.

John Bell took to his bed in 1820. His son found a nearly empty bottle of strange-looking medicine. The son heard the witch cackle, "I've got him this time."

When the doctor arrived at the house, he tested the unknown medicine by giving some to the cat, who died immediately. The next day, John Bell was also dead!

The witch then declared to the family, "I am going and will be gone for seven years." After that, all was calm in the Bell household.

Seven years later the noises began again. By this time, Betsy and most of the other children had already married and moved away. The noises were ignored by the rest of the family and ended after two weeks.

The strange story of the Bell witch was discussed in detail in a book written by John Bell's son Richard in 1846. What makes this case unusual is that most recorded poltergeists do not harm their victims. They may be annoying and playful, throwing dishes and moving furniture around, but they normally stop short of physical attack.

Did the witch, who seemed to get most of her energy from Betsy, torment and then kill John Bell because the young girl resented her father? If so, then why did the witch also torment Betsy? And how could she have returned to the Bell home seven years later if Betsy had already moved away?

One expert believes a house with nine children, many of them teenagers, provided plenty of energy for a particularly cruel and malicious poltergeist. The children were unhappy and disliked their very strict and disciplinary father.

The case of the Bell witch stands out as an exception among poltergeist incidents—one that will hopefully never be repeated.

Redsy

Ever since Redsy was a puppy, she would go with her master everywhere. The Irish setter especially loved to go on fishing trips. She enjoyed riding in her master's boat off the New England coast and was never bothered by the occasional choppiness and rough seas of the Atlantic Ocean.

On one particular day, her master, William Montgomery, had just finished stocking his boat. He was looking forward to a great day of flounder fishing. The weather couldn't have been more perfect; there wasn't a single cloud in the beautiful blue sky.

"Let's shove off, Redsy," said Montgomery. "Those fish are waiting for us."

Usually the dog needed little encouragement to

jump into the boat, but today was different. Redsy refused to move. She sat on shore and stared at her master.

"What's wrong with you, girl?" asked Montgomery. "Get in the boat!"

Redsy stood up and barked, but she refused to move off the dock.

"Come, Redsy," Montgomery commanded. "I said, into the boat."

But the more he insisted, the louder Redsy barked. It was obvious that the dog did not want anything to do with this particular fishing trip.

"I can't figure you out, Redsy. You always love to go fishing," declared Montgomery. "What's bothering you, girl?"

The man scratched his head and thought for a while. He stared out to sea and saw dozens of other fishermen heading toward the flounder banks in their boats.

For an instant, Montgomery considered going out alone and leaving the dog behind on the dock. But never in his memory could he recall Redsy acting so strangely. He remembered some of his friends saying that his dog had more sense than most people they knew. Montgomery figured that something wasn't right.

Maybe Redsy knows something I don't, he thought to himself. "Okay, girl, you win!" he said out loud. "The trip's off. Let's go home! It wouldn't have been fun without you anyway."

The dog jumped up and ran around excitedly in circles, relieved at the news.

An hour later, the beautiful blue sky was full of storm clouds. Without warning, galelike winds blew in from the sea. Enormous waves battered the New England coast, destroying beach cottages and smashing small boats. Some waves were almost forty feet high!

Of the fifty boats that set out that day to fish for flounder, few made it back to shore. More than six hundred people were killed. Years later, they called it the great hurricane of 1938!

That evening, William Montgomery gave Redsy an extra-special dinner. He even let her sit on his favorite chair. He didn't know how or why, but the dog had sensed the impending danger of the storm. Redsy had known that if they had set out to sea, they would probably never come back.

Was it extrasensory perception? Can a dog have a premonition or vision of danger? Was it animal instinct?

Whatever it was, William Montgomery knew full well that Redsy had saved his life. And for that, he was always grateful.

Ghost of a Young Man

Kathy was washing dishes in the kitchen of her new one-story home. Suddenly a shadow crossed the window. She glanced up from the sink and saw a young man walking by.

"Hello, can I help you?" she called to the stranger, who was rather shabbily dressed. He was heading toward the rear of her house.

Drying her hands, Kathy hurried to the back door to intercept him. Looking out, she saw the man walk slowly through the backyard garden and toward the large hedge that marked the end of the property. Then he disappeared! Kathy looked around, but there was no sign of the stranger!

Over the next month, she saw him many times, always dressed in the same shabby clothes. He walked in the same direction into the garden, his head down. Sometimes he passed through the hedge into the field beyond before he disappeared. Other times he vanished in the garden or near the kitchen window.

Kathy was sure she was seeing a ghost and finally told her husband, Bob. He chuckled after hearing her story.

I can tell he doesn't believe me, thought Kathy. Maybe he thinks I'm imagining it all. I even wonder that myself.

The man appeared to Kathy two or three times a week, but sometimes he showed up several times a day. In one twenty-four-hour period, she saw him walk the same route at least seven times!

One weekend, Kathy's mother was visiting Kathy and Bob. "Where's that young man I saw walking to the back of the house?" her mother asked.

"What young man?" replied Bob. "There's no one here."

When her mother described the stranger, it matched the description of the ghost Kathy had been seeing for weeks.

At least I'm not going out of my mind, Kathy thought. Someone else has seen him, too!

Bob finally believed Kathy. But soon afterward, just as suddenly as the ghostly man appeared, he disappeared for many months. So much time passed that Kathy and Bob forgot all about the strange intruder.

Then one morning, almost a year later, he appeared again.

"He came last October," Kathy declared, "and now he's here again this October!"

"We've got to get to the bottom of this," said Bob.

He went to the Institute of Psychical Research for help. After an investigation, researchers discovered that the house had once been part of a larger farm. There had been a path that ran near the house, through the garden and hedge, and into the field. A pond had been located in the middle of the field.

The owners of the farm had a son who attended the local university. The young man became very depressed and kept to himself. His parents didn't know how to help him feel better. The young man would often take long walks alone along the path, with his head down. He always seemed to be deep in thought as he walked.

One day in October, the farmer's son took his customary walk. But this time, when he got to the pond, he jumped in and drowned.

Every October, the ghost of the young man returns to retrace the final footsteps of his life. Over and over again, he walks until the month ends, and then he returns the following year.

Although Kathy and Bob understood the sad reason for this haunting, they never really felt comfortable with it. Eventually, they sold their home and moved away.

The Drums of Death

"This is a wonderful dinner, Lady Airlie," said the woman visitor to her gracious hostess as they enjoyed a lavish meal. "Thank you so much for inviting me to be your guest at Cortachy Castle."

"The pleasure is ours, madame," replied the smiling hostess.

The visitor paused, then said, "A strange thing occurred as I was dressing for dinner a short time ago."

"Do tell us, dear," said an interested Lord Airlie.

"Well," the woman began, "I heard music outside my window. Actually, it was the sound of a drummer playing near the castle."

Suddenly, all activity ceased at the dinner table.

The other guests cleared their throats and acted embarrassed. Lord Airlie turned as white as a ghost, and his wife looked very upset.

Oh dear, what have I said? thought the woman to herself. She decided to quickly change the subject. "The weather is quite lovely at this time of year in Scotland, don't you think? In London, it's still so damp and cold." Eventually the conversation started up again and things appeared to return to normal.

Later that evening, the woman was determined to find out what had made everyone so distressed at her mention of the drumming. Another guest explained to her that the castle was haunted by the ghost of a drummer boy. Many years ago, the boy angered a former lord. As punishment, the boy was forcibly pushed into his drum and thrown out of the castle tower to his death. Before he was killed, the boy had threatened to haunt the family forever. Since then the drum was reportedly heard before the deaths of several different family members.

"In fact, the drum was heard before the late Countess of Airlie died unexpectedly in her sleep several years ago," explained the guest.

The next day, the woman again heard the sounds of the drummer. She decided to leave the castle and visit friends in nearby Dundee. Apologizing to Lord and Lady Airlie, the woman was relieved to leave. She never wanted to hear those drums again!

Within hours, Lady Airlie was dead. She had left a note explaining that she knew the drum was sounding for her. Five years later, the drums were heard again when Lord Airlie was on a hunt. The following day, he was dead.

Thirty years passed. The music of the drums was heard again at Cortachy Castle. The current Lord Airlie was in the United States at the time and was not even aware that the drums were sounding. An hour later, he was dead.

Does the ghostly music of the drums foretell a death in the family? Are the people so terrified of the drums that they actually die of fright because they believe their time on Earth is up?

The twelfth Earl of Airlie died in 1968. His widow claims the drums were not heard by anyone prior to his death. Is the curse of the ghostly drummer boy finally over? Or was it all just a series of bizarre coincidences? Only time will tell.

The Lady in White

"Oh, no!" screamed Alex as he slammed his foot down hard on the brake. He had been driving along eastbound highway A677 on the way to Blackburn, in Lancashire, England, when a woman had run out of nowhere right in front of his car. He felt a sickening thud as the automobile hit the woman's body and then ran over her.

"My God, what did we hit?" exclaimed Alex's wife, who wasn't paying attention when the woman ran into the road.

As the car screeched to a stop, Alex couldn't keep himself from shaking.

"I think I've killed someone," he said, his voice thick with emotion. "I've got to find out if she's still alive."

Alex hurriedly got out of the car. He looked underneath and then behind the car, but there was no sign of a body. He searched up and down the road and off the shoulder on both sides but found nothing.

He returned to the car, shaken and confused. "She was wearing a long white gown," he told his wife, "and I know I hit her. It's like she just disappeared into thin air!"

This mysterious incident took place in 1987. More than forty other similar incidents have been reported over the years on this same highway. All drivers claimed to have hit a woman in white, but they could not find a body.

Not far from the scene of these "nonaccidents" is Samlesbury Hall, reportedly haunted by the ghost of Lady Dorothy Southworth. As the story goes, about four hundred years ago Lady Dorothy, a Roman Catholic, fell deeply in love with a Protestant boy. Because of their religious differences, the couple was forbidden by their families to see each other.

They continued to meet in secret, however, and one day made plans to elope. Unfortunately, Dorothy's brothers overheard the couple's plans. When her lover came to take her away, the brothers killed him and his companion, then secretly buried the bodies on the grounds of Samlesbury Hall.

When Lady Dorothy heard the news, she was heartbroken and died soon afterward from grief.

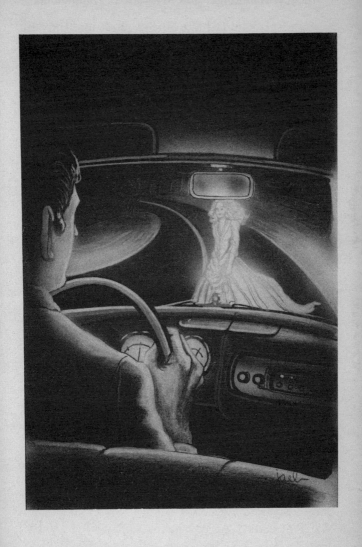

Her ghost is said to haunt the grounds and the hall itself.

In the early nineteenth century, the skeletons of two men were reportedly discovered near the hall. It is not certain whether these are the remains of Lady Dorothy's lover and his friend.

Over the years, people have reported seeing the ghost of Lady Dorothy, dressed all in white, and many have heard her crying. She has sometimes been seen walking among the trees outside the hall.

Drivers claim they have seen her by the side of the road. Some have stopped to offer her a ride, but when they approach her, she mysteriously disappears.

Is the strange apparition really the ghost of the heartbroken Lady Dorothy? Or could there be some other explanation as to why so many drivers have reported seeing a mysterious woman in white? Can these sightings be a mass hallucination or overactive imaginations at work? You be the judge.

Bridey Murphy

"Keep your eyes on the candle flame," said hypnotist Morey Bernstein to his subject, Ruth Simmons.

It was Saturday, November 29, 1952. Bernstein was attempting age-regression hypnosis. While the subject was in a hypnotic trance, he would take her back in time to when she was a youngster, and then farther back to when she was an infant.

In this particular attempt, Bernstein wanted to keep on going and try to take the woman back to the time *before* her birth to see if any memories existed.

"You will fall into a deeper and deeper sleep," Bernstein explained to his subject as she remained in a trance. "Now we are going to turn back time and space, and when I next talk to you, you will be seven years old, and you will answer my questions."

Ruth responded to questions first as a seven-year-old then as a five-year-old, a three-year-old, and a one-year-old.

"Now I want you to keep on going back and back in your mind," continued Bernstein. "Keep going back until you find yourself in some other scene at some other time. You will be able to talk to me about it and answer my questions."

After several minutes, Bernstein asked, "How old are you?"

"Eight," the subject replied.

"Now that you are eight years old, do you know what year it is?" the hypnotist asked softly.

"1806," she declared.

"What is your name?"

"Bridey . . . Bridey Murphy," answered the subject.

In a series of five interviews, all recorded on tape, Bernstein questioned his subject about nineteenth-century Ireland, where Bridey Murphy said she lived. Ruth had never been to Ireland, but as Bridey she revealed specific details of Irish life nearly a hundred years earlier.

According to Ruth, Bridey was born in 1798 and lived in the town of Cork. She was the daughter of Duncan and Kathleen Murphy. Bridey married

Brian McCarthy and moved to Belfast, where she died at age sixty-six in 1864.

The case of Bridey Murphy received much publicity in the 1950s. Bernstein wrote a best-selling book about it and the tape recordings of the hypnosis sessions were sold.

Many attempts were made to find out if Bridey Murphy really existed. Unfortunately, no birth or death records were kept that far back in Ireland.

During Bernstein's interviews, Bridey mentioned the names of two grocers in Belfast from whom she bought food. One was Mr. Farr and the other was John Carrigan. A Belfast librarian found a city directory for 1865–1866 that listed both men as grocers.

Does this prove reincarnation is real? Are people reborn after death into new lives? Have we all lived as different people in the past? Or did Ruth, under hypnosis, completely fantasize the character of Bridey Murphy?

Although many case details were found to be correct, some people believed that Ruth's memories as Bridey were actually taken from Ruth's own childhood remembrances. Ruth's aunt, Marie Burns, was Irish, but she grew up in New York, not Ireland. An Irishwoman named Bridey Corkell lived across the street from Marie and her husband. Did the details of Bridey Murphy's life, as well as her first name, come from this neighbor?

Many people have had experiences that they feel

they have been through before. The French call it *déjà vu*. Does *déjà vu* prove that reincarnation exists, or is it just a memory of a similar scene in our present life that has been forgotten?

There are no definite answers to the case of Bridey Murphy and the question of reincarnation. The search to solve the mystery continues. Is the end really a new beginning? No one knows for sure.

Flight to Nowhere

"James, I'm taking a Camel to Tadcaster Airfield," said Lieutenant David M'Connel to his friend, Lieutenant James Larkin. "I expect to be back in time for tea. Cheerio!"

Both young men were pilots stationed at Scampton Airfield in Lincolnshire, England. It was a December morning in 1918.

David planned to fly the sixty miles to Tadcaster to make a delivery in his Sopwith Camel biplane. He sat in an open cockpit behind twin machine guns, goggles over his eyes.

The Camel was a fragile airplane by today's standards. Its wings were made of wood and fabric. It stood only 8½ feet high and was less than 19 feet long!

James spent the afternoon writing letters and reading in front of the fire, waiting for David to return. At about 3:30 P.M., the door opened and David stepped into the room.

"Hello, old boy," he said to James, who turned to face his friend.

James saw David standing in the doorway, dressed in his flying clothes. His cap was pushed back on his head, and he was smiling.

"Hello. Back already?" asked James.

"Yes," David replied. "Got there all right and had a fine trip. Well, cheerio!" He turned and left.

David went on reading. About fifteen minutes later, a pilot friend came into the room and said, "I hope M'Connel gets back early. We're going to Lincoln this evening."

"But he *is* back," James declared. "He was here just a few minutes ago."

"I'll try and find him," said the pilot.

It wasn't until later that evening that James heard the awful news. David and another flyer had been caught in a thick blanket of fog on the way to the Tadcaster field. The other man made a forced landing, but David continued on, trying to get through the fog and stay at a safe altitude.

A short distance from Tadcaster, the Camel, which had a reputation as a difficult plane to fly, went into a nosedive. It crashed, and David was killed when his head struck one of the machine guns in front of the cockpit. His watch was recov-

ered from the wreckage. It had stopped at 3:25 P.M.

"That's almost precisely the time I saw David in the room," declared an astonished James.

"Perhaps you were mistaken about David and the time," said his pilot friend. "Maybe you dreamed the whole episode."

"I was definitely wide awake, and I know what time it was," insisted James. "David looked so normal and yet, I must have seen him at the exact moment of his death!"

In a letter to David's father, James wrote: "I am of such a skeptical nature regarding things of this kind that even now I wish to think otherwise—that I did not see him—but I am unable to do so."

Did James simply imagine the meeting with David? Or did he see the ghost of his friend, who had returned to talk with him just one last time?

What do *you* think?

Glossary

CLAIRVOYANCE: the ability to identify or become aware of an object, person, or event without using the five basic senses (sight, hearing, smell, taste, and touch).

COINCIDENCE: occurrences of events that seem related but are not actually connected.

CURATOR: the person in charge of a museum, zoo, library, or other exhibit.

DÉJÀ VU: the feeling that something has been experienced before.

DEMONOLOGIST: an expert on the supernatural and the spirit world.

DOWSING: to search for a water or mineral source using a special stick or rod.

ELECTROMAGNETIC: magnetism that is produced by a current of electricity.

EXORCISM: a special ceremony used to cast out evil spirits and demons.

EXTRASENSORY PERCEPTION (ESP): special abilities and knowledge that extend beyond the normal five senses.

FLINTLOCK: a seventeenth- or eighteenth-century gun in which the powder is exploded by a spark produced when a flint strikes a metal plate.

HALLUCINATION: seeing people or things that aren't really there.

KNOTS: a ship's speed. A knot is one nautical mile per hour.

LEVITATION: the lifting up or floating of a medium or others at a séance.

MEDIUM: a person who communicates with the dead.

PAYLOAD: the cargo of a vehicle.

PHENOMENA: extraordinary or unusual occurrences.

POLTERGEIST: a noisy or mischievous ghost that often moves objects from place to place.

PRECOGNITION: the knowledge of events before they actually happen.

PREMONITION: an advance warning of an event; similar to precognition.

PSYCHIC: a person who is sensitive to supernatural forces.

REINCARNATION: the belief that a person's soul is reborn in a new human body after death.

SCAVENGER: someone who collects or uses discarded or leftover objects.

SÉANCE: a sitting with a medium to contact otherworldly spirits.

SUPERNATURAL: anything caused by other than the known forces of nature.

Bibliography

Arvey, Michael. *Reincarnation*. San Diego, Calif.: Greenhaven Press, 1989.

Barrett, Sir William, and Theodore Besterman. *The Divining Rod*. New Hyde Park, N.Y.: University Books, 1968.

Bernstein, Morey. *The Search for Bridey Murphy*. Garden City, N.Y.: Doubleday, 1956.

Bro, Harmon Hartzell. *A Seer Out of Season: The Life of Edgar Cayce*. New York: New American Library, 1989.

Broughton, Richard S. *Parapsychology: The Controversial Science*. New York: Ballantine, 1991.

Brown, Raymond Lamont. *Phantoms of the Theater*. Nashville: Thomas Nelson, 1977.

Bibliography

Brown, Rosemary. *Unfinished Symphonies*. New York: William Morrow, 1971.

Cohen, Daniel. *Phone Call from a Ghost*. New York: G. P. Putnam's Sons, 1988.

Cohen, Daniel. *The Ghosts of War*. New York: G. P. Putnam's Sons, 1990.

Constable, George, ed. *Ghosts*. Alexandria, Virg.: Time-Life Books, 1984.

Constable, George, ed. *Psychic Powers*. Alexandria, Virg.: Time-Life Books, 1987.

Constable, George, ed. *Phantom Encounters*. Alexandria, Virg.: Time-Life Books, 1988.

Constable, George, ed. *Visions and Prophecies*. Alexandria, Virg.: Time-Life Books, 1988.

Curran, Robert. *The Haunted*. New York: St. Martin's Press, 1988.

Day, James Wentworth. *In Search of Ghosts*. New York: Taplinger, 1970.

Fairley, John, and Simon Welfare. *Arthur C. Clarke's World of Strange Powers*. New York: G. P. Putnam's Sons, 1984.

Gardner, Colin B., ed. *Ghostwatch*. London, England: Foulsham, 1989.

Gauld, Alan, and A. D. Cornell. *Poltergeists*. London, England: Routledge & Kegan Paul, 1979.

Bibliography

Halifax, Viscount Charles Lindley. *Lord Halifax's Ghost Book*. Secaucus, N.J.: Castle Books, 1986.

Hall, Trevor H. *New Light on Old Ghosts*. London, England: Gerald Duckworth & Co. Ltd., 1965.

Holzer, Hans. *Ghost Hunt*. Norfolk, Virg.: Donning Company Publishers, 1983.

Kettlekamp, Larry. *Mischievous Ghosts*. New York: William Morrow, 1980.

Knight, David C., ed. *The ESP Reader*. New York: Grosset & Dunlap, 1969.

MacManus, Diarmuid. *Between Two Worlds*. Gerrards Cross, Buckinghamshire, England: Colin Smythe Ltd., 1977.

Marsden, Simon. *The Haunted Realm*. New York: Dutton, 1986.

May, Antoinette. *Haunted Houses of California*. San Carlos, Calif.: Wide World Publishing/Tetra, 1990.

McHargue, Georgess. *Facts, Frauds, and Phantasms*. Garden City, N.Y.: Doubleday, 1972.

Myers, Arthur. *Ghosts of the Rich and Famous*. Chicago: Contemporary Books, 1988.

Prince, Walter Franklin. *Noted Witnesses for Psychic Occurrences*. New Hyde Park, N.Y.: University Books, 1928.

Reynolds, James. *Ghosts in Irish Houses*. New York: Bonanza Books, 1957.

Bibliography

Roberts, Nancy. *Haunted Houses*. Chester, Conn.: Globe Pequot Press, 1988.

Shoemaker, John Bruce, Ben Williams, and Jean Williams. *The Black Hope Horror*. New York: William Morrow, 1991.

Smith, Susy. *Haunted Houses for the Millions*. Los Angeles: Sherbourne Press, 1967.

Stemman, Roy. *Spirits and Spirit Worlds*. London, England: Danbury Press, 1975.

Stevens, Austin N. *Mysterious New England*. Dublin, N.H.: Yankee, 1971.

Tabori, Paul. *Harry Price: The Biography of a Ghost Hunter*. New York: Living Books, 1966.

Taylor, L. B. Jr. *Haunted Houses*. New York: Julian Messner, 1983.

Underwood, Peter. *A Gazetteer of Scottish and Irish Ghosts*. New York: Walker and Company, 1973.

Walker, Danton. *I Believe in Ghosts*. New York: Taplinger, 1969.

Warren, Ed and Lorraine, with Robert David Chase. *Ghost Hunters*. New York: St. Martin's Press, 1989.

Westbie, Constance, and Harold Cameron. *Night Stalks the Mansion*. Harrisburg, Penn.: Stackpole Books, 1978.

Wilson, Colin. *Poltergeist*. New York: G. P. Putnam's Sons, 1981.

Wylder, Joseph Edward. *Psychic Pets*. New York: Stonehill, 1978.

TOR CLASSICS

☐☐	50510-7 50511-5	THE WIND IN THE WILLOWS *Kenneth Grahame*	$2.50 Canada $3.25
☐☐	50482-8 50481-X	ROBINSON CRUSOE *Daniel Defoe*	$2.50 Canada $3.25
☐☐	50502-6 50503-4	STORIES BY O. HENRY *O. Henry*	$2.50 Canada $3.25
☐☐	50442-9 50443-7	DRACULA *Bram Stoker*	$2.50 Canada $3.25
☐☐	50420-8 50421-6	THE ADVENTURES OF TOM SAWYER *Mark Twain*	$2.50 Canada $3.25
☐☐	50422-4 50423-2	THE ADVENTURES OF HUCKLEBERRY FINN *Mark Twain*	$2.50 Canada $3.25
☐☐	50428-3 50429-1	BLACK BEAUTY *Anna Sewell*	$2.50 Canada $3.25
☐☐	50483-6 50484-4	THE SCARLET LETTER *Nathaniel Hawthorne*	$2.50 Canada $3.25
☐☐	50457-7 50458-5	FRANKENSTEIN *Mary Shelley*	$2.50 Canada $3.25
☐	50501-8	THE SECRET GARDEN *Frances Hodgson Burnett*	$2.50 Canada $3.25
☐	55754-9	THE WAR OF THE WORLDS *H.G. Wells*	$2.95 Canada $3.95
☐☐	50508-5 50509-3	TREASURE ISLAND *Robert Louis Stevenson*	$2.50 Canada $3.25

Buy them at your local bookstore or use this handy coupon:
Clip and mail this page with your order.

Publishers Book and Audio Mailing Service
P.O. Box 120159, Staten Island, NY 10312-0004

Please send me the book(s) I have checked above. I am enclosing $ _____
(Please add $1.25 for the first book, and $.25 for each additional book to cover postage and handling.
Send check or money order only—no CODs.)

Name _____

Address _____

City _____ State/Zip _____

Please allow six weeks for delivery. Prices subject to change without notice.